THE
ROOFTOP
MYSTERY

THE
ROOFTOP
MYSTERY

by JOAN M. LEXAU

Pictures by SYD HOFF

An I CAN READ Book®

■ HarperCollins*Publishers*

TO JANEEN HAAS

It was moving day for Sam.

He was moving four blocks away.

Albert was helping.

Iris began to cry.

"Sam, carry her doll,"

his mother said.

"But she carries it around

all the time," Sam said.

"Why not now?"

9

Sam's father said,

"Iris is tired and cross.

We are all busy.

Carry the doll, Sam."

So Sam carried the doll.

He gave his plane to Albert to carry.

Sam's mother carried the baby

and a dish that had been her mother's.

12

Sam's father carried the big clock
and a box of things that might break.
Iris did not carry anything.

They went out the door.

"Can Albert and I ride in the van?"
Sam asked.

"I will ask the men if you may,"

his mother said. "Oh, dear,

did I turn out all the lights?"

"I will go look," Sam said.

17

He and Albert went back in.

All the lights were out.

"My mother does that too," Albert said.

"Does what?" asked Sam.

"Thinks she hasn't turned things off
when she has," Albert said.

They went out again and shut the door.

The car was gone. The van was gone.

Sam looked at Albert.

Albert looked at Sam.

They both looked at the doll.

20

"Maybe I had better carry the plane,"

Sam said.

Albert said, "Oh, no.

I am not going to carry that big doll."

"Well, I am not walking four blocks

with this stupid doll," said Sam.

People were walking by.

He put the doll behind him.

They tried to get back inside,

but the door had locked behind them.

"I know what," Albert said. "We can go

down the street to Amy Lou's building.

We can go up on the roof

and think what to do."

They ran to the building.

The door to the roof was open.

Sam said, "Albert, if you laugh

we will never be friends again."

"Why should I laugh?" Albert said.

He began to shake and cough.

Sam hit him on the back to stop him.

When he could talk, Albert said,

"Maybe Amy Lou

will carry the doll for us.

You found her jump rope for her

the other day. Maybe she will remember."

"Yes, but I was the one who hid it.

Maybe she will remember that too.

But we will have to ask her to help.

What else can we do?" said Sam.

"She will laugh
if she sees me with the doll.
You stay here with it,
and I will ask Amy Lou."
Albert said, "No, you stay here,
and I will go ask her.

26

I am not going to stay here

with a doll."

"Let's both go, then,

and leave the doll here," Sam said.

They went to Amy Lou's apartment
and told her about the doll.

"I will be glad to help," Amy Lou said,

"as soon as I get back."

"When will that be?" Albert asked.

"Next week," Amy Lou said.

"I'm going to my grandmother's."

"You are a big help," Sam said.

Amy Lou looked out the window.

"Anyway, I would not go out
in this rain," she said.

"Rain!" Sam said.

"Man, that's all we need."

As they ran up the stairs,

Albert said, "Why does Iris

have to have such a big doll!"

"She thinks it is real," Sam said.

"She talks to it and sings to it,

and she can't sleep without it.

She would even bring it to dinner,

if my father would let her."

They ran out on the roof to where

they had left the doll.

It was gone.

"Somebody took it!" Sam said.

"Look around some more," said Albert.

Sam said, "It did not walk away.

This is where we left it."

He looked down at the street far below.

"Hey, there it is!" he yelled.

"That girl has it."

"Run!" Albert said.

"We can catch up with her."

They ran down to the street.

"There she is," Albert said.

They ran down the block after the girl.

Sam grabbed the doll's arm.

"This is my little sister's," he said.

"I don't care if you found it.

You give it back."

The doll began to yell

and kicked Sam in the stomach.

"You leave my little sister alone,"
the girl said.

"Oops, sorry," said Sam.

"You big bully!" said the girl.

"He is not," Albert said.

"From far away she looked like
his little sister's doll."

"I wish she was a doll.

She is so heavy, and she cries when

I don't carry her," the girl said.

Amy Lou ran up to them.

"I just looked for you on the roof.

I'm going now, but I will take the doll

on my way to the bus," she said.

"The doll is gone. Could I call

the police on your phone?" Sam asked.

"Sure. I think I can find the number

for you," Amy Lou said.

Sam called the police.

"I left a doll on a roof

and it is gone," he said.

"Can you find out who took it?"

A policeman said, "Is this a joke,

or did someone really take your dolly,

little girl?"

Sam said, "It's not my dolly—

I mean doll. And I am a brother—

I mean a boy."

38

"Oh," said the policeman.

"Well, let me talk to your mother."

"I will call you back," Sam said.

He hung up the phone.

As the boys left, Amy Lou said,

"I would have carried it, Sam.

I just said No at first.

But I would have helped you."

"That's okay, Amy Lou," Sam said.

"Thanks anyway."

They did not know where to go,

so they went back to the roof.

"I hope you find your dolly, Sam,"

Amy Lou called after them.

"Girls!" Sam said.

"Now Iris won't be able to sleep.

My mother will be mad at me.

My father will be mad at me.

Maybe I should run away.

Could I stay at your place?"

"Sure," Albert said. "But my mother

will tell your mother where you are.

Why not try to find the doll?"

"This is where we left it," Sam said.

"It must be far away by now."

Albert said, "Look around.

Maybe somebody moved the doll.

Or maybe there is a clue someplace."

They looked all over, again and again.

There was no doll and no clue.

"Can Iris get a new doll?"

Albert asked.

"It wouldn't be the same," said Sam.

"Girls are funny about dolls.

It's not like getting a new baseball.

How will I tell her I lost her doll?"

Sam took a last look at the roof.

"Wait. There is something different about the roof. It isn't like it was when we left the doll here," he said.

"What is different?" asked Albert.

"Something—" Sam said. "I know. There were clothes on the lines then.

Does that help? No."

"Maybe you could get Iris a doll
just like the old doll," Albert said.

"Wait, I am thinking," said Sam.

"There were clothes on the lines
when we left the doll here.

I think they were gone
when we came back for it.

So somebody took the clothes down
and maybe saw who took the doll."
"Maybe," Albert said, "but how can we
find out who took down the clothes?
Hey, we can go to every door and ask.
It must be somebody in this building."
So they did, starting on the top floor.
One lady slammed the door on them
when they asked, "Did you wash today?"
One lady on the third floor
said she had washed clothes.

"At last!" Albert said.

"Did you see a doll?"

"Why would I have seen a doll?"
the lady asked.

47

"When you took down the clothes,
did you see a doll?" asked Sam.

"But I did not take down the clothes,"
the lady said. "They are still hanging
in the kitchen."

"Oh," Sam said. "You didn't hang them
on the roof?"

"No, it looked too much like rain,"
the lady told them.

"Thanks anyway," Sam said.

They kept on knocking at doors.

A lady on the first floor said

that she had washed clothes.

"Did you hang them on the roof?"

asked Albert.

"And did you see a doll?" asked Sam.

The lady said, "Yes, I did and I—"

"Did you see who took it?" Sam asked.

"Yes, I know who took it,"

the lady said.

"Who?" Sam and Albert said
at the same time.

"I did," the lady said.

"I did not want such a nice doll to get
rained on, so I took it with me.

I hung my clothes up in the kitchen.

Later I went upstairs to ask Amy Lou

if she knew whose doll it was.

But there was no one home."

She asked them to come in

and gave Sam the doll.

"Thanks a lot. Am I glad to see it!

I don't even mind so much

about carrying it home now.

Let people laugh," said Sam.

"I see. You did not want to carry it

down the street," the lady said.

Sam told her about moving

and about getting stuck with the doll.

Albert said, "If we only had

a big bag or a box to carry it in."

Sam was looking at a clothesbasket.

Should he ask if they could use it?

The lady saw him looking at it.

"Go ahead. I know you boys," she said.

"I have seen you playing around here.

You can bring the basket back

in the morning."

"Gee, thanks," Sam said.

The lady put some newspaper

on top of the doll.

Sam and Albert ran all the way

to Sam's new building

and went up to the second floor.

There were four doors.

"Hey," said Sam.

"Hey what?" said Albert.

"I forget the number," Sam said.

"Well, we can start knocking

on doors again," Albert said.

"No, I have a better way," Sam said.

"MOTHER!" he yelled.

Sam's father let them in.

"Sam Bunting, where have you been?
You should have been here helping,
not outside playing," he said.

"He wasn't playing, Mr. Bunting,"
Albert said. "Really he wasn't."

Sam said, "When we came out,
you were gone and the van was gone."

"Oh, dear," his mother said.

"I forgot to ask about the van.

The baby was crying so hard.

58

I am sorry, Sam.

Then we had to tell the men

where to put things.

And Iris has been so cross

about something.

I have been too busy to think."

She looked around.

"Dear me," she said,

"I seem to have two clothesbaskets.

But that cannot be."

Sam gave the doll to Iris.

She smiled at him.

"Well, there we were—" Sam said.

His father said, "Albert's mother

asked us over for dinner.

You can tell us about it on the way."

They got ready to go out

and went down the stairs.

"Where is Iris?" Mr. Bunting asked.

They all looked back at Iris.

"That doll is too heavy

for her to carry so far,"

Mrs. Bunting said.

"Oh, no," Sam yelled.

"Not again! Come on, Albert. Run."

"What is the matter, Sam?"

asked Mr. Bunting.

But Sam and Albert were far away.

64